# LION NEEDS A SHOT

## Hyewon Yum

ABRAMS BOOKS FOR YOUNG READERS
NEW YORK

For Emma and Hana

The illustrations for this book were made with colored pencils.

Cataloging-in-Publication Data has been applied for
and may be obtained from the Library of Congress.

ISBN 978-1-4197-4829-5

Text and illustrations © 2022 Hyewon Yum
Book design by Hana Anouk Nakamura

Printed and bound in China
10 9 8 7 6 5 4 3 2 1

Abrams Books for Young Readers are available at special discounts
when purchased in quantity for premiums and promotions as well as fundraising
or educational use. Special editions can also be created to specification.
For details, contact specialsales@abramsbooks.com or the address below.

Abrams® is a registered trademark of Harry N. Abrams, Inc.

**ABRAMS** The Art of Books
195 Broadway, New York, NY 10007
abramsbooks.com

Well, we're seeing Dr. Brown today.

Uh-oh. Why?

Just for a checkup
to see that everything is fine.

You're a big lion.
I know you'll be all right.

I'm just worried about Lulu.

No worries, Dad! She'll be OK.
I'll be there with her the whole time.

Great! Great!

By the way, you're not going to bite
Dr. Brown's finger this time, are you?

Definitely not.

Last time it was just
my extra-sharp tooth.

I didn't bite at all.

Don't worry, Lulu.

Dr. Brown will only press your tongue for a few seconds.

I'm not worried.

And Dr. Brown always warms up her stethoscope.

OK.

Hi, I'm Nurse Bill!

Could you step up here for me, please?

Lulu, he's checking
how much you grew.

I grew more than you!

Now read the chart, and
tell Nurse Bill what you see.

I know.

When Dr. Brown touches your tummy, it tickles a lot.

You don't like tickling, right?

Aw, I'm so worried about you.

Why? That doesn't tickle me at all.

And we need shots.
They keep you from getting sick!

After you get a shot,
you get a really nice sticker.

I love stickers!
I want a rainbow one.

Come to think of it, I don't need to see a doctor today.
Look at me! I'm perfectly fine.

Hey there.

It's nice to see you,
Luka and Lulu.

Oh, I think our little lion
needs more time.

Does Lulu want to go first?

No problem. I'll go first.

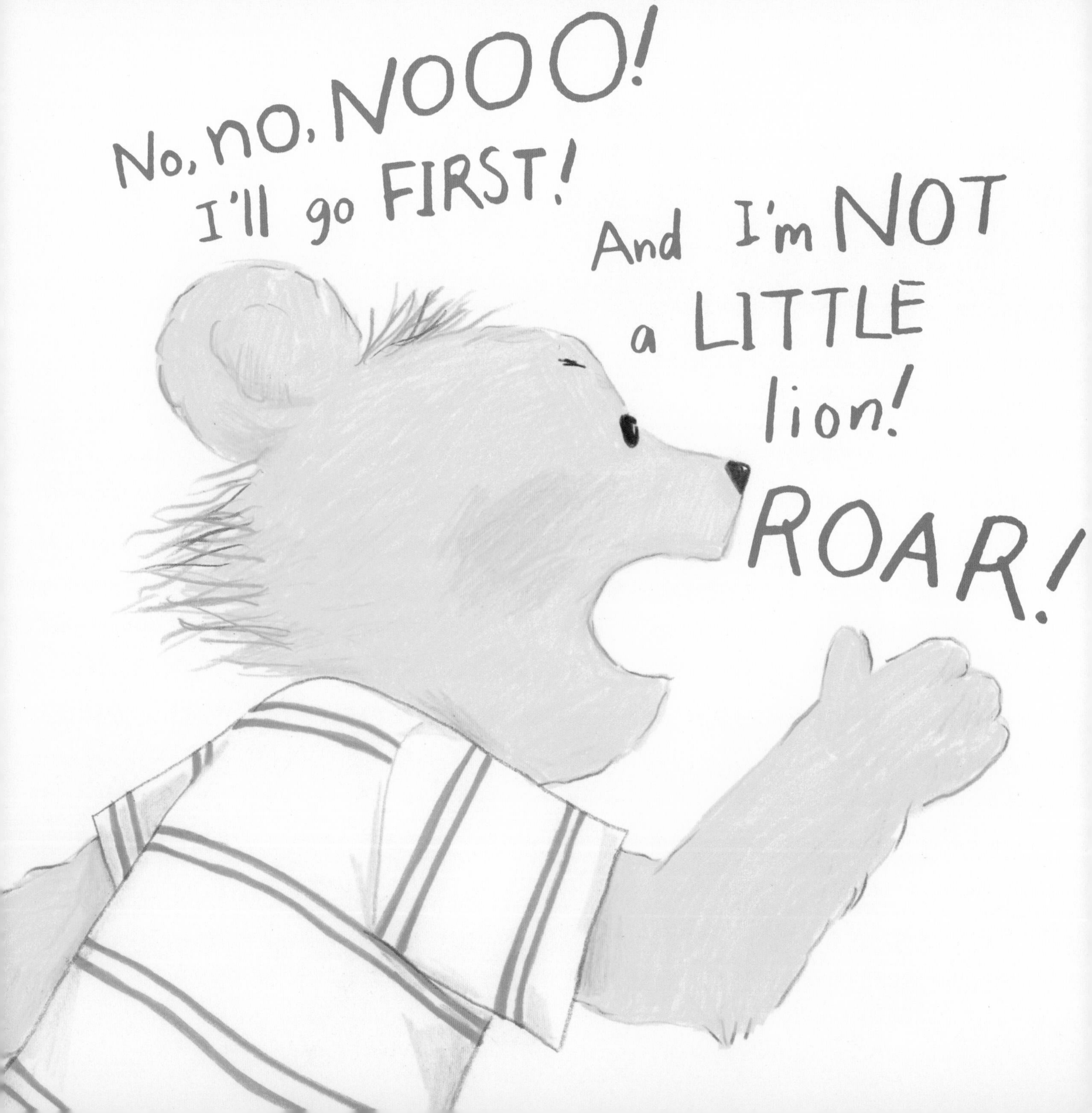
No, no, NOOOO!
I'll go FIRST!
And I'm NOT
a LITTLE
lion!
ROAR!

Oh my, you are really big now!

My bad!

Lulu, just look at me
and you'll know what to do.

See, you open your mouth BIG!

Stay still.

Make sure you don't blink.

Lulu, it doesn't tickle.

Don't worry.

Take a deep breath.

You're doing great!

Now it's time for a shot.

Lulu, it's OK.

Think about what you like best.

It only takes a few seconds.

Ouch!

Wow! You're such a good big brother.

Do you think Lulu will be a big lion just like you?

You'll be fine, Lulu.
I'll hold your hand.

Oh, Lulu. Now it's all done.
You are a big lion, just like me!

That wasn't bad at all.

See, Lulu?
You got the coolest sticker!

I'm so proud of you kids.

I'm not sure I could get a shot like you did.

Dad, you don't look well.

I think you need to see the doctor.

You have nothing to worry about!

I'll hold your hand when you get a shot.